To Jack and Lois Walburg,
*My parents, mentors, and best friends.*
—LW


To Maddie, Joel, Eliot, Hayla, & Daisy,
*May the story of the candy cane and the truth of Christ's love live in your hearts.*
—RC

ZONDERKIDZ

*The Legend of the Candy Cane*
Copyright © 1997 by Lori Walburg
Illustrations © 2012 by Richard Cowdrey

Requests for information should be addressed to:

Zondervan, 5300 Patterson Ave SE, Grand Rapids, Michigan 49530

Library of Congress Cataloging-in-Publication Data: Applied for
Walburg, Lori.
    The legend of the candy cane / by Lori Walburg and Richard Cowdrey.
        p.   cm.
    Summary: With the help of young Lucy, a mysterious stranger called Mr. Sonneman tells the
story of the candy cane to the people of a small prairie town during Christmas time at the turn of
the century. Includes a history of the candy cane.
    ISBN 978-0-310-73012-5 (hardcover : alk. paper)  [1. Candy canes--Fiction. 2. Christmas--
Fiction. 3. Jesus Christ--Nativity--Fiction.]  I. Cowdrey, Richard, ill. II. Title.
PZ7.W1337Le 2012
 [E]--dc23                                                          2011035001

*Editor: Barbara Herndon*
*Art direction and design: Kris Nelson*

*Printed in China*

# The Legend of the Candy Cane

## The Inspirational Story of Our Favorite Christmas Candy

WRITTEN BY *Lori Walburg*

ILLUSTRATED BY *Richard Cowdrey*

ZONDERVAN.com/
AUTHORTRACKER
*follow your favorite authors*

One dreary evening in the depths of November a stranger rode into town. He stopped his horse in front of a lonely storefront. The windows were boarded shut and the door was locked fast. But the man looked at it, smiled, and said, "It will do."

All through the short, gray days and the long, dark nights of November, the man worked.

The townspeople could hear the faint *pam pam pam* of his hammer and the *snish snish snish* of his saw.

They could smell the sweet, clean scent of new lumber and the deep, oily smell of new paint.

But no one knew who the man was or what he was doing.

The mayor hoped the man was a doctor, to heal his illness. The young wives hoped he was a tailor, to make beautiful dresses. The farmers hoped he was a trader, to exchange their grain for goods.

But the children had the strongest, deepest wish of all. A wish they did not tell their parents. A deep, quiet, secret wish that none of them said out loud.

No one spoke to the man. No one asked if he needed help. They just waited. And watched. And wondered. And wished.

FLOUR

OATS

But one small girl watched and wondered, waited and wished longer than she could stand. And one snowy day she knocked at the stranger's door. "Hello," she said. "My name is Lucy. Do you need some help?"

The man smiled warmly and nodded. Then he opened the door, and Lucy stepped inside.

A long counter ran down the side of the room. Bare shelves filled the opposite walls. In the back were dozens and dozens of barrels and crates.

"Could you help me unpack?" the man asked.

Lucy's heart sank at the sight of all the boxes. What if they were only barrels of nails and bags of flour?

But she removed her dripping boots and hung her coat on a peg. On stocking feet, she crossed the rough wooden floor and knelt beside a crate.

"Please. Open it," the man urged.

Slowly, Lucy put her hand into the box and pulled out an object wrapped in tissue. Round and heavy, it almost slipped through her fingers. Lucy trembled a little as she unwrapped it.

It was a glass jar.

Lucy gave the man a puzzled look. "Go on," his nod said.

So she unpacked another glass jar, and another, and another, until she was completely surrounded by jars of all shapes and sizes. Tall and thin. Round and squat. Jars with lids and jars without.

"Now," the man said, "for something to put inside." And he pulled over a huge crate stamped with a strange word.

As Lucy unpacked, her eyes lit up.

It was candy. Her favorite candy. Gumdrops!

"Try some," the man said.

She popped one in her mouth. Now she could hardly unwrap fast enough. Peppermint sticks! Taffy! Lollipops! Chewing gum!

Wide-eyed, she looked at the man.

"We wished—," Lucy said.

"Yes, I know," said the man. "And here it is. Welcome to Sonneman's Candy Store. I am John Sonneman."

Soon the small store was filled with candies, gleaming in their glass jars. Raspberry suckers and tiny lemon drops. Brightly colored jawbreakers and long tangles of licorice. Pink and white peppermints for church and butterscotch balls for company.

Then, in the very last package in the very last crate, was a candy Lucy had never seen before, a red-and-white striped candy stick with a crook on the end.

"What is this?" Lucy asked.

"This," Mr. Sonneman explained, "is a candy cane. It is a very special Christmas candy."

"Why?" Lucy asked.

"Tell me," Mr. Sonneman said, "what letter does it look like?"

Lucy took the candy and turned it in her hand.

"J!" she said.

"Yes." Mr. Sonneman smiled. "J for Jesus, who was born on Christmas day."

"Now, turn it over. What does it remind you of?"

Lucy turned the candy in her hand. She peered down intently. "I know!" she said finally. "It's like a shepherd's staff."

"Who were the first to find out about Jesus' birth?" Mr. Sonneman asked.

"Shepherds in the field," Lucy answered, "watching over their flocks by night."

"But Mr. Sonneman, what are the stripes for?" Lucy asked.

The man's eyes grew sad. "The prophet Isaiah said, 'By his stripes we are healed.' Before he died on the cross, Jesus was whipped. He bled terribly. The red reminds us of his suffering and his blood."

"But then," Mr. Sonneman continued, "the candy is white as well. When we give our lives to Jesus, his blood washes away our sins, making us white and pure as snow."

"That," he said, "is the story of the candy cane."

"Is it a secret?" Lucy asked.

Mr. Sonneman looked at her for a long moment. "It's a story that needs to be told," he said. "Will you help me share it?"

It was now the depths of December. The town was whipped round by blizzard winds. For days, the sun hid itself.

But every morning, Mr. Sonneman and Lucy ventured out. They wore heavy woolen coats and bright handknit scarves. And in their stiff, mittened fingers, they each held a bag.

They went to every house in town. They traveled to every farm in the country. They knocked on every door. In every home, they told the story, they left a small gift, and they gave an invitation.

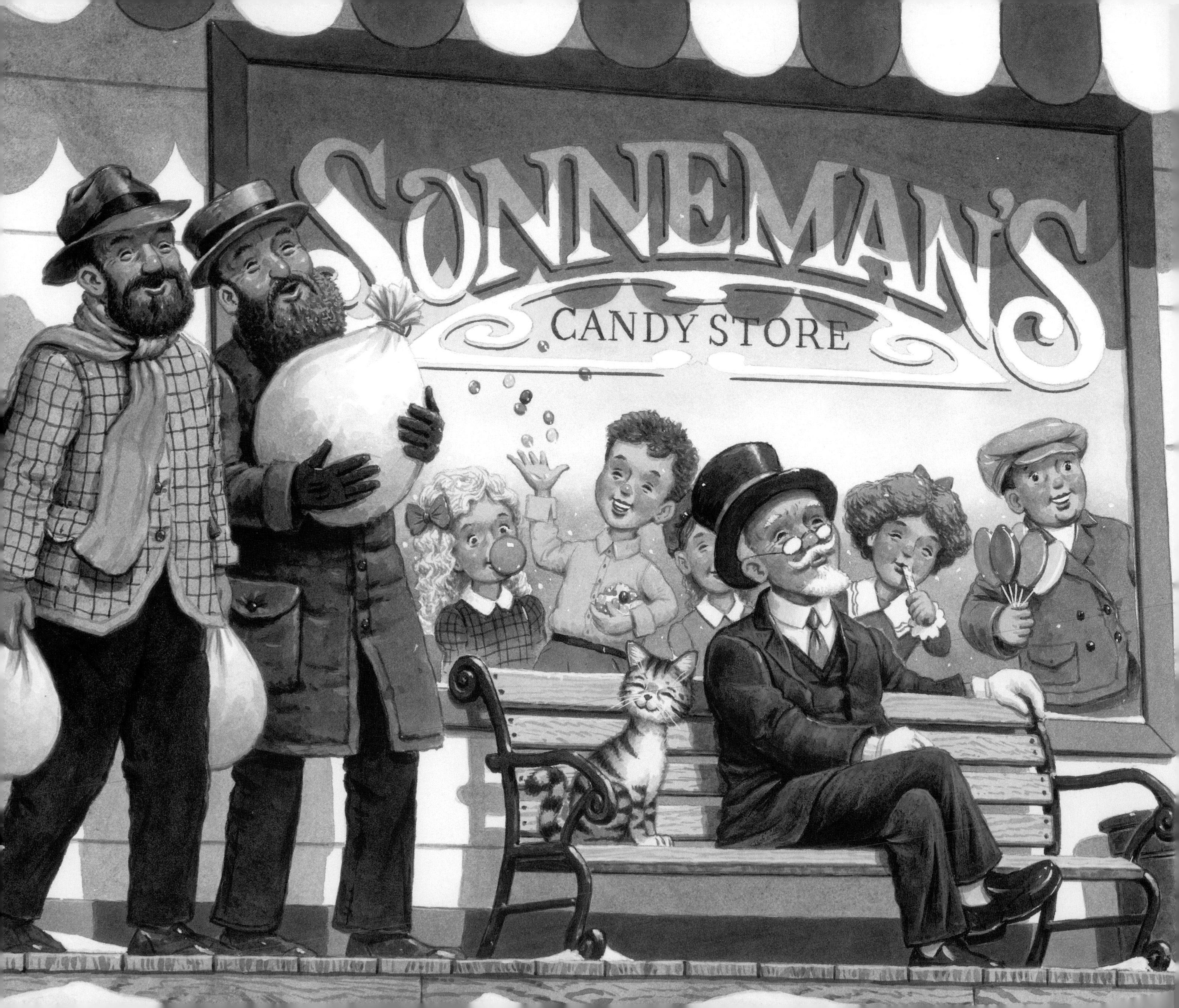
SONNEMAN'S
CANDY STORE

On the afternoon of Christmas Eve, the sun finally broke through the clouds.

And Sonneman's Candy Store officially opened.

The mayor came, feeling better than he'd felt in days. The young wives came, dressed in beautiful smiles. The farmers came, eager to trade grain for Christmas gifts. The children ran in dizzy circles.

Yes, their wish had come true.

Yes, they had come to share in the opening of the candy store.

But they shared something more. Something bigger. Something better.

On that Christmas Eve, they shared the story of the candy cane.

They told the miracle of Christ's birth.

The misery of his death.

And the mercy of his love.

# The History of the Candy Cane

The traditional candy cane was born over 350 years ago when mothers used white sugar sticks as pacifiers for their babies. Around 1670, the choirmaster of Cologne Cathedral in Cologne, Germany, bent the sticks into canes to represent a shepherd's staff. He then used these white candy canes to keep the attention of small children during the long Nativity service.

The use of candy canes during the Christmas service spread throughout Europe. In northern Europe, sugar canes decorated with sugar roses were used to brighten the home at Christmas time.

In the mid 1800s, the candy cane arrived in the United States when a German-Swedish immigrant in Wooster, Ohio, decorated his spruce tree with paper ornaments and white sugar canes.

The red stripe was added to the candy cane at the turn of the century, when peppermint and wintergreen were added and became the traditional flavors for the candy cane. Some sources say that a candy maker in Indiana developed the candy cane as a witness of Christ's love. While we may never know the full history of the candy cane, we can share in the truth behind its symbol, the truth of Christ's birth and redemption, and the gift of his love.